Tails of the Red Panda

OUT OF THE WOODS

Story by

Robert Padan

Illustrated by

Jack McCoy

totrp.com

Copyright © 2020 Robert Padan

All rights reserved.

ISBN:

Dedicated to the Brave Men and Women of the United States Navy

Tails of the Red Panda

OUT OF THE WOODS

The ginger sailor pushed his cart, bucket, and swab through the hatch into the female head, calling out as he entered "Male on deck". No one replied so he, hung the maintenance sign on the hatch, entered and began cleaning toilets.

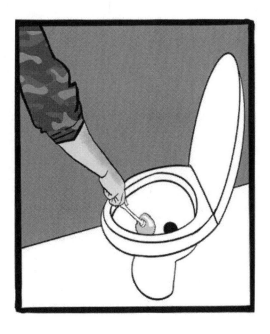

Someone entered the head and spoke "I'd recognize that tail anywhere."

The ginger sailor jumped up from his hands and knees banging his head on the door of the toilet stall as he did so, turning he saw his friend and asked, "Medi, what are you doing here?"

"Well captain obvious, this is the female head, and you may have noticed I am female, and I have business to take care of."

About two years earlier... The perky Medi Doore and the shy Ginger met at the navy recruiting office while they were both university students.

Both were on scholarship, academic for the Ginger and athletic for Medi, but were bored and looking for adventure, so they each found the recruiter. They recognized each other from common classes. Started talking and agreed that school was boring, and the Navy offered adventure. The Ginger said he was going to try out for the SEALS. Medi said she was going for the SEALS also.

"Girls can't join the SEALS." Ginger protested.

"Yes, they can." Medi answered, "As of January 2016."

"Really!"

"Yes, really, did you ever read a newspaper, or the notice on that bulletin board?" Medi said while pointing at the bulletin behind him.

"Oh." Then two doors opened, and the recruiters motioned them each into their offices.

They finished their interviews at about the same time, and both started for the food court, then Medi suggested, "Let's go get a beer?"

"I can't drink any beer. I have to lose

weight."

"I have to gain weight." Medi laughed. "This place in the mall serves beer and burgers. You can have a salad."

"Ok, the recruiter told me I should start working out... Uhhmmm... Do you want to be training partners?" Ginger offered shyly.

"Yeah, I can barely swim. Do you know anything about swimming?"

"OH YEAH...District champion in the 500 freestyle." The Ginger said brightly.

They went in the mall restaurant and sat at the bar. Medi ordered beer and a burger and fries, and got carded, while the Ginger ordered diet water and a salad.

"You're older than you look." The ginger said surprised.

"You're not supposed to say that to a lady; didn't your mother teach you anything?"

"Sorry. It's just that when you got carded..."

Medi smiled saying, "Don't worry about it. I'm used to it. I'm at school on a gymnastics scholarship and being small helps, but I'm too old for the Olympics and school is getting old, so I want to do something different, so when the politicians told the Navy they had to accept girls into SEALS training...I went for it.

I think I can handle the fitness and training, ya'know those gymnastics coaches are basically sadists, worse than any trainers in the military, but I really need help with swimming, so if you really mean we can be training partners…" "YOU BETCHA'," the

Ginger enthusiastically agreed, thinking about hanging out with this gorgeous gymnast. She was petite and well-tanned, dark haired and dark eyed, with well-proportioned muscles; and he imagined her healthy body in a well fitted bathing suit…, he grabbed his fork and stabbed his hand to refocus his wandering mind, as their food arrived.

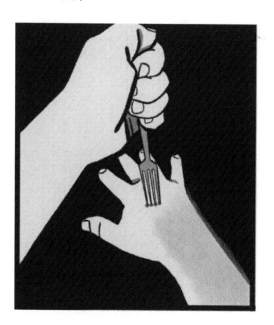

"You must be very hungry?" Medi commented with a curious expression.

"Starving!" In more ways than one Ginger thought.

They finished their meal and agreed on a workout schedule. The workouts went well. Medi struggled; her small frame and lack of body fat gave her the natural buoyancy of a stone.

The Ginger was woefully out of shape, but he was young enough that hard work would pay off, but Medi was afraid of the water.

At the campus pool, "Don't fight it." Ginger advised. "Watch this." He took several deep breaths in rapid succession, then blew it all out, fell forward and slowly sank to the bottom of the dive well. It was twelve feet deep. He stayed down. He stayed down a long, long, long time. Medi looked at the clock on the wall. He stayed down. She looked at the clock again, more than two minutes had passed. He stayed down. Finally, he slowly rose to the surface.

A lifeguard had come over. When he surfaced the lifeguard told him seriously, "If you try that stunt again in my pool without telling me, you will be banned."

"Yeah right, sorry about that, I was just trying…"

"I don't care what kind of showing off you were up to; you had just better let me know what's going on." The lifeguard stalked off.

"He's right, but anyway, what did you think?" The Ginger smirked.

"That was scary; I didn't think you were coming back up."

"It's a trick, all biology and chemistry and physics. Most people can hold their breath a lot longer than they think they can, but they panic and burn up all of their oxygen. When I hyperventilated ya'know, took all those deep breaths before I went down, I purged my blood of carbon dioxide and loaded up on oxygen. When I was down, I forced myself to relax and counted very slowly to two hundred. I used to be able to make it to three hundred. But I forgot that it really freaks out the lifeguards, should have told him, sometimes they won't let you do it. But I know that guy; he's seen me here before."

"Three Hundred! That would be almost five minutes." Medi was astonished.

"You can do it too."

"How?"

"Control your fear. Don't get me wrong, fear can be a good thing. It makes you respect danger, but you can learn to control it. Let's do an exercise. We'll go to the shallow end and see if you can hold your breath to a ten count." "I can do more than ten." Medi protested.

"Baby steps."

As they passed the lifeguard station, they told him what they were doing. He didn't say anything but nodded and gave them a hard look.

They got in the shallow end. Medi started taking deep breaths, then blew out her air, and sank to the bottom. She counted to twelve then started to feel panic and stood up, panting.

"Not bad, now do the same thing but on your last lungful take it in as deep as you can and hold your breath."

She did but floated and made it to fifteen. "I floated."

"You are the master of the obvious. The kind of swimming we have to prepare for is more about endurance, buoyancy and breath control, than pure speed, you'll get it." She stuck her tongue out at him.

They made progress. Medi gained a little weight and got better at swimming. Ginger lost weight and got more fit. Medi asked, "How did your parents take it when you told them?"

"Uhhmmm, I haven't actually told them yet. What did your parents say?"

"Wweelll, my mom freaked out, like she thought I was going to be some great Olympic gymnast, but my dad was more understanding and thought it was a pretty good idea. He told me that less than one percent of one percent of Olympic athletes actually make enough money to live on as athletes. You have to tell your parents; you know they're going to find out anyway."

"Yeah, I know, but it will be my dad who

freaks out and my mom who understands." He called that night and he was right.

They continued working out, including jogging through the park which included the state zoo.

They still had their School ID cards so they got in free, walking around the exhibits as part of their cool down. A pair of red pandas was in a new temporary exhibit near the entrance.

The Ginger was drawn to it. Medi looked back and forth from her friend to the pandas. "You have the same hair."

The Ginger continued to stare at the pandas. The pandas stopped chewing on bamboo and approached the bars of their cage, stood up on their hind feet and leaned on the bars with their hand-like paws. Ginger approached, put his hands on the bars and stared at the pandas as they stared at him.

"Hello, Ginger are you there, is anybody home?"

Ginger continued staring.

People started noticing. "Ginger, people are looking at you."

Ginger continued staring. The Ginger and the Red Pandas each laid hands on the other's heads.

"Dost, thou aspire to the mantle of a warrior?" A voice spoke in the Ginger's mind.

"Yes, who are you?"

"A messenger from the Creator,

and a warrior. Might this one give thee some advice?"

"Yes."

"The adversary is powerful. Thou will not defeat thine opponent with strength alone. Use stealth, intelligence, guile and cunning.

The Creator offers thee a gift. These creatures seen before thee, thou will be able to take on this appearance, yet thine human substance remains unchanged."

"I begin to see messenger; these Red Pandas are stronger than they appear. Although their diet is mainly plant, they retain the teeth and claws of a carnivore. They appear soft and endearing yet they are tough, fast and can be fierce. It is an excellent talent the Creator bestows."

"Beware the temptation of self-righteous rage young warrior. Thou and thy friend will soon be tested. Anger is a sin and a

weakness. If action is called for be swift and overwhelming, it is more kind to overcome thy foe quickly than to allow the contest to linger. Seek guidance from holy men and women. Thou will recognize them."

"Will I remember your words messenger?"

"As in a dream."

"Are you connected to these animals?"

Medi asked nervously.

The Ginger and the pandas slowly turned their heads in unison and looked at Medi. The pandas went back to chewing bamboo. "Did you say something?"

"I said that you have the same hair as these red pandas. Are you somehow connected?"

"Well of course, all Gingers share a spiritual connection." He said with a wink, then walked away to finish their cool down, Medi followed.

They made it through boot camp at Great Lakes. Ginger helped others learn to swim, then more specialized training at Great Lakes, then Coronado, California.

Medi was right when she compared sadistic gymnastic coaches with SEAL trainers.

When they were sent to Maine for SERE training something happened that would change their lives.

On his way to Maine, the Ginger visited a small country church. While sitting on a bench outside he was approached by an old man with some ginger left in his hair that had gone gray. "Good morning young man. I am the pastor here. May I join you?"

"Of course."

"You look like one of those sailors going to the wilderness training."

"Yes, it can't be worse than anything I've been through so far."

"You never know, just remember God has put his mark on you," and the old pastor laid his hands on the Ginger's red head and prayed.

Some of the trainers in Maine were not active duty navy. In a new experimental development, civilian contractors were used for parts of the training, learning how to live off the land. They were led by members of Community Reformers Environmental Education Patrol, who had a mixed code of ethics, such as claiming to be for equal rights for women while many of their members had criminal records for domestic abuse, but their political connections got them the job.

They were just supposed to educate them about wild foods available in various seasons and environments, but they exceeded their authority going beyond that to do individual overnight wilderness encounters. The CREEPs had their students go out in the woods individually then they would dart them with drugs to try to frighten them. After all their training it took more than some stupidhead, tree hugging, druggie weirdos to scare these recruits, but many of the trainees had bad reactions to the drugs.

Medi selected her campsite and tried to make it as inconspicuous as possible. She had seen the Ginger setting up camp nearby and spied on him.

As she watched he stripped off his t-shirt and pants, so he was only wearing black boxers. Then he started to wash himself.

During their training, the men did not shave or wash much so she understood his need to be clean.

She was surprised by his appearance. Ginger had matured, with his short beard; the Ginger was covered in hair. It was all red on top and became darker on his body blending with his black boxers. She had seen him shirtless before but in the long months of training he had nearly grown a fur coat. She felt attracted to the raw wild nature of his pelt, it made him look manly.

As she watched he was approached by two of the civilian trainers.

One of whom held up a long tube and grinned.

As one of them raised the tube to his mouth Ginger reached out for it, while the other clubbed his arm with a baseball bat, breaking the outstretched arm. She had never heard the Ginger raise his voice and swear like he did as he told the CREEPs what they could do with their tubes and clubs. Then from behind her she heard an aggressive voice, "Lookie here boys I found a girl."

She swung around and started punching and kicking but her assailant was too far away and armed with what looked like another long tube held up to his mouth. She felt a small sting, then went limp.

The drug took away all of her muscle control, but she could still see and hear. The CREEP shouted, "I got her first but you'uns can have sloppy seconds." Then he started stripping off his pants.

Another of the CREEPs shouted, "Don't forget to give her the roofies so she won't remember. As this CREEP was distracted the Ginger dove into him grabbing the bat with his good arm.

Medi watched, paralyzed by the drugs. Her attacker looked up, his companions were reeling from a vicious attack as the Ginger tore into them, first with the bat, then teeth and claws, until they were bleeding and unconscious on the forest floor. Her attacker stared as what looked to him like a large red raccoon or a small red bear leapt onto him. He stumbled in his dropped pants and the animal started biting and clawing everywhere, until he also was a bloody unconscious mess..

With the attackers subdued, the animal sniffed at Medi and determined she was paralyzed but unharmed. He stayed with her for hours. While he waited another CREEP approached. The CREEP saw the bloody aftermath and started to approach. The Red Panda advanced toward the stalker with stealth.

Unseen by the intruder, the animal growled inhumanly, "Leave while you still can."

The CREEP soiled his pants and ran off tripping over himself in the forest, quite unlike a wilderness expert.

The Ginger Sailor gently made her comfortable then picked her up as gently as he could with his injured arm, growling, "I will keep you safe". As darkness fell he carried her back to base.

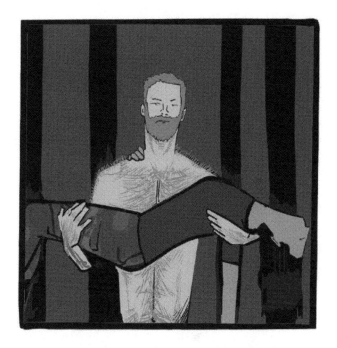

Medi recovered, her attackers would never be the same. She finished her training and became the first female SEAL in Navy history. She had no idea what happened to her friend until she ran into him in the female head.

The ginger sailor jumped up from his hands and knees banging his head on the door of the toilet stall as he did so,

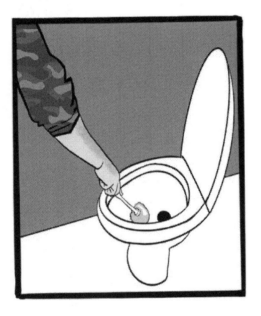

turning he saw his friend and asked, "Medi, what are you doing here?"

"Well captain obvious, this is the female head, and you may have noticed I am female, and I have business to take care of...what are you doing here?"

"I still have three years left on my commitment."

"What happened in Maine? I was paralyzed, but I could see and hear everything."

"What did you see?"

"You turned into an animal and beat the holy crap out of those CREEPs."

"Did you tell anyone?"

"No, I passed out after a while and after a whole day and night, the CREEPs were dead, I guess, and when the drugs wore off I woke up back at the base and was told I had passed all the training. They never questioned me on what happened back in the woods."

"Good, never tell anyone what you saw, I told the Navy you were unconscious and had no idea what happened. They want to pretend the whole thing never happened."

"What happened to the CREEPS?"

"Let's just say they have returned to

nature."

"What do you mean?"

The Ginger sighed heavily and uttered quietly, "I cut a deal with the Navy. I'm out of the SEALS, and I still have to finish my commitment, but I will get an honorable discharge and regular benefits. I can't talk about it, but that stupidhead deputy assistant secretary of the navy, Peyton Roberts, who got his jerk CREEP cousins all those contract trainer jobs, is gone and his stupid experiment is over too."

"What kind of deal?"

"You are going to have an exciting career, which will bring honor to you and peace and security to our country; you will be looked out for."

"What about you?"

"I have toilets to clean. There's another female head down the companionway, all clean and shiny. I believe you have business to take care of, and I have promises to keep."

Hey Kids Check These Out

(888) 943-1534

https://www.goarmy.com/

(888) 673-9123

https://www.navy.com/

(800) 423-USAF

https://www.airforce.com/

(800) MARINES

https://www.marines.com/

See your local recruiter.

https://www.gocoastguard.com/

Made in the USA
Columbia, SC
21 December 2020